RANDOM HOUSE

LARGE PRINT

Also by Paulo Coelho
Available from Random House
Large Print

Hippie

The Archer

Paulo Coelho

The Archer

Illustrations by Christoph Niemann
Translated by Margaret Jull Costa

RANDOM HOUSE
LARGE PRINT

The Library of Congress has established a
Cataloging-in-Publication record for this title.

ISBN: 978-0-593-34253-4

www.penguinrandomhouse.com/
large-print-format-books

FIRST LARGE PRINT EDITION

Printed in the United States of America

10 9 8 7 6 5 4 3 2 1

This Large Print edition published in accord
with the standards of the N.A.V.H.

To Leonardo Oiticica, who, one morning, upon seeing me practice judo at Saint-Matin, gave me the idea for this book.

O Mary! conceived without sin,
pray for us who turn to you!
Amen.

A prayer without a deed is an arrow without a bowstring;

A deed without a prayer is a bowstring without an arrow.

—Ella Wheeler Wilcox

Contents

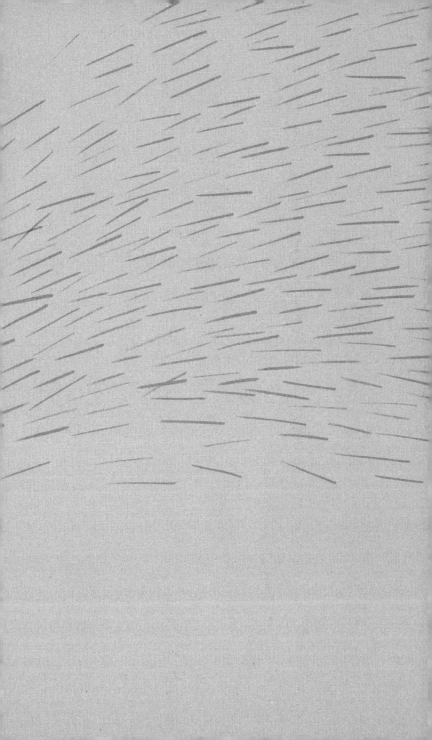

PROLOGUE

"Tetsuya."

The boy looked at the stranger, startled.

"No one in this city has ever seen Tetsuya holding a bow," he replied. "Everyone here knows him as a carpenter."

"Maybe he gave up, maybe he lost his courage, that doesn't matter to me," insisted the stranger. "But he cannot be considered to be the best archer in the country if he has abandoned his art. That's why I've been traveling all these days, in order to challenge him and put an end to a reputation he no longer deserves."

The boy saw there was no point in arguing; it was best to take the man to the carpenter's shop so that he could see with his own eyes that he was mistaken.

Tetsuya was in the workshop at the back of his house. He turned to see who had come in, but his smile froze when his eyes fell on the long bag that the stranger was carrying.

"It's exactly what you think it is," said the new arrival. "I did not come here to humiliate or to provoke the man who has become a legend. I would simply like to prove that, after all my years of practice, I have managed to reach perfection."

Tetsuya made as if to resume his work: he was just putting the legs on a table.

"A man who served as an example for a whole generation cannot just disappear as you did," the stranger went on. "I followed your teachings, I tried to respect the way of the bow, and I deserve to have you watch me shoot. If you do this, I will go away and I will never tell anyone where to find the greatest of all masters."

The stranger drew from his bag a long

bow made from varnished bamboo, with the grip slightly below center. He bowed to Tetsuya, went out into the garden, and bowed again toward a particular place. Then he took out an arrow fletched with eagle feathers, stood with his legs firmly planted on the ground, so as to have a solid base for shooting, and with one hand brought the bow in front of his face, while with the other he positioned the arrow.

The boy watched with a mixture of glee and amazement. Tetsuya had now stopped working and was observing the stranger with some curiosity.

With the arrow fixed to the bowstring, the stranger raised the bow so that it was level with the middle of his chest. He lifted it above his head and, as he slowly lowered his hands again, began to draw the string back.

By the time the arrow was level with his face, the bow was fully drawn. For a moment that seemed to last an eternity, archer and bow remained utterly still. The boy was looking at the place where the arrow was pointing, but could see nothing.

Suddenly, the hand on the string opened, the hand was pushed backward, the bow in the other hand described a graceful arc, and the arrow disappeared from view only to reappear in the distance.

"Go and fetch it," said Tetsuya.

The boy returned with the arrow: it had pierced a cherry, which he found on the ground, forty meters away.

Tetsuya bowed to the archer, went to a corner of his workshop, and picked up what looked like a slender piece of wood, delicately curved, wrapped in a long strip of leather. He slowly unwound the leather and revealed a bow similar to the stranger's, except that it appeared to have seen far more use.

"I have no arrows, so I'll need to use one of yours. I will do as you ask, but you will have to keep the promise you made, never to reveal the name of the village where I live. If anyone asks you about me, say that you went to the ends of the earth trying to find me and eventually learned that I had been bitten by a snake and had died two days later."

The stranger nodded and offered him one of his arrows.

Resting one end of the long bamboo bow against the wall and pressing down hard, Tetsuya strung the bow. Then, without a word, he set off toward the mountains.

The stranger and the boy went with him. They walked for an hour, until they reached a large crevice between two rocks through which flowed a rushing river, which could be crossed only by means of a fraying rope bridge almost on the point of collapse.

Quite calmly, Tetsuya walked to the middle of the bridge, which swayed ominously; he bowed to something on the other side, loaded the bow just as the stranger had done, lifted it up, brought it back level with his chest, and fired.

The boy and the stranger saw that a ripe peach, about twenty meters away, had been pierced by the arrow.

"You pierced a cherry, I pierced a peach," said Tetsuya, returning to the safety of the bank. "The cherry is smaller. You hit your target from a distance of forty meters, mine was half that. You should, therefore, be able to repeat what I have just done. Stand there in the middle of the bridge and do as I did."

Terrified, the stranger made his way to the middle of the dilapidated bridge, transfixed by the sheer drop below his feet. He performed the same ritual gestures and shot at the peach tree, but the arrow sailed past.

When he returned to the bank, he was deathly pale.

"You have skill, dignity, and posture," said Tetsuya. "You have a good grasp of technique and you have mastered the bow, but you have not mastered your mind. You know how to shoot when all the circumstances are favorable, but if you are on dangerous ground, you cannot hit the target. The archer cannot always choose the battlefield, so start your training again and be prepared for unfavorable situations. Continue in the way of the bow, for it is a whole life's journey, but remember that a good, accurate shot is very different from one made with peace in your soul."

The stranger made another deep bow, replaced his bow and his arrows in the long bag he carried over his shoulder, and left.

On the way back, the boy was exultant.

"You showed him, Tetsuya! You really are the best!"

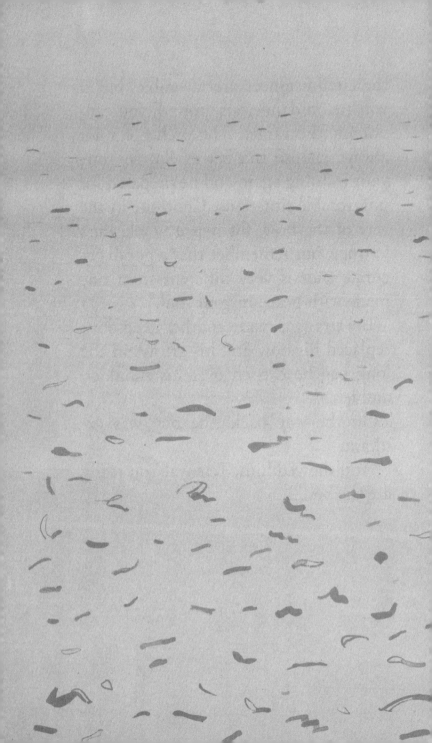

"We should never judge people without first learning to hear and to respect them. The stranger was a good man; he did not humiliate me or try to prove he was better than I am, even though he may have given that impression. He wanted to show off his art and to have it recognized, even though it may have appeared that he was challenging me. Besides, having to confront unexpected trials is part of the way of the bow, and that was precisely what the stranger allowed me to do today."

"He said that you were the best, and I didn't even know you were a master archer. So why do you work as a carpenter?"

"Because the way of the bow serves for everything, and my dream was to work with wood. Besides, an archer who follows the way does not need a bow or an arrow or a target."

"Nothing interesting ever happens in this village, and now suddenly here I am, face-to-face with the master of an art that no one even cares about anymore," said the boy, his eyes shining. "What is the way of the bow? Can you teach me?"

"Teaching it isn't hard. I could do that in less than an hour, while we're walking back to the village. The difficult thing is to practice it every day, until you achieve the necessary precision."

The boy's eyes seemed to be begging him to say yes. Tetsuya walked in silence for nearly fifteen minutes, and when he spoke again, his voice sounded younger:

"Today I am contented. I did honor to the man who, many years ago, saved my life, and, because of that, I will teach you all the necessary rules, but I can do no more than that. If you understand what I tell you, you can use those teachings as you wish. Now, a few minutes ago, you called me master. What is a master? I would say that he is not someone who teaches something, but someone who inspires the student to do his best to discover a knowledge he already has in his soul."

And as they came down the mountain, Tetsuya explained the way of the bow.

ALLIES

The archer who does not share with others the joy of the bow and the arrow will never know his own qualities and defects.

Therefore, before you begin anything, seek out your allies, people who are interested in what you are doing.

I'm not saying "seek out other archers." I'm saying: find people with other skills, because the way of the bow is no different from any other path that is followed with enthusiasm.

Your allies will not necessarily be the kind of dazzling people to whom everyone looks up to and of whom they say: "There's none better." On the contrary, they are people who are not afraid of making mistakes and who do, therefore, make mistakes, which is why their work often goes unrecognized. Yet they are just the kind of people who transform the world and, after many mistakes, manage to do something that can make a real difference in their community.

They are people who can't bear to sit around waiting for things to happen in order to decide which attitude to adopt; they decide as they act, well aware that this could prove highly dangerous.

Living with such people is important for an archer because he needs to realize that before he faces the target, he must first feel free enough to change direction as he brings the bow up to his chest. When he opens his hand and releases the string, he should say to himself: "As I was drawing the bow, I traveled a long road. Now I release this arrow knowing that I took the necessary risks and gave of my best."

The best allies are those who do not think like everyone else. That is why when you seek companions with whom you can share your enthusiasm for archery, trust your intuition and pay no attention to what anyone else may say. People always judge others by taking as a model their own limitations, and other people's opinions are often full of prejudice and fear.

Join with all those who experiment, take risks, fall, get hurt, and then take more risks. Stay away from those who affirm truths, who criticize those who do not think like them, people who have never once taken a step unless they were sure they would be respected for doing so, and who prefer certainties to doubts.

Join with those who are open and not afraid to be vulnerable: they understand that people can improve only once they start looking at what their fellows are doing, not in order to judge them, but to admire them for their dedication and courage.

You might think that archery would be of no interest to, say, a baker or a farmer, but I can assure you that they will introduce whatever they see into what they do. You will do the same: you will learn from the good baker how to use your hands and how to get the right mix of ingredients. You will learn from the farmer to have patience, to work hard, to respect the seasons, and not to curse the storms, because it would be a waste of time.

Join with those who are as flexible as the wood of your bow and who understand the signs along the way. They are people who do not hesitate to change direction when they encounter some insuperable barrier, or when they see a better opportunity. They have the qualities of water: flowing around rocks, adapting to the course of the river, sometimes forming into a lake until the hollow fills to overflowing, and they can continue on their way, because water never forgets that the sea is its destiny and that sooner or later it must be reached.

Join with those who have never said: "Right, that's it, I'm going no further," because as sure as spring follows winter, nothing ever ends; after achieving your objective, you must start again, always using everything you have learned on the way.

Join with those who sing, tell stories, take pleasure in life, and have joy in their eyes, because joy is contagious and can prevent others from becoming paralyzed by depression, loneliness, and difficulties.

Join with those who do their work with enthusiasm, and because you could be as useful to them as they are to you, try to understand their tools too and how their skills could be improved.

The time has come, therefore, to meet your bow, your arrow, your target, and your way.

THE BOW

The bow is life: the source of all energy.

The arrow will leave one day.

The target is a long way off.

But the bow will stay with you, and you must know how to look after it.

It requires periods of inaction—a bow that is always armed and braced loses its strength. Therefore, allow it to rest, to recover its firmness; then, when you draw the bowstring, the bow will be content, with all its strength intact.

A bow has no conscience: it is a prolongation of the hand and desire of the archer. It can serve to kill or to meditate. Therefore, always be clear about your intentions.

A bow is flexible, but it has its limits. Stretching it beyond its capacity will break it or exhaust the hand holding it. Therefore, try to be in harmony with your instrument and never ask more than it can give.

A bow is at rest or under tension in the hand of the archer, but the hand is merely the place where all the muscles of the body, all the intentions of the archer, and all the effort of shooting are concentrated. Therefore, in order to maintain elegance of posture while keeping the bow drawn, make sure that every part does only what is necessary and do not dissipate your energies. That way, you will be able to shoot many arrows without tiring.

In order to understand your bow, it must become part of your arm and an extension of your thoughts.

THE ARROW

The arrow is the intention.

It is what unites the strength of the bow with the center of the target.

The intention must be crystal clear, straight and balanced.

Once the arrow has gone, it will not come back, so it is better to interrupt a shot, because the movements that led up to it were not sufficiently precise and correct, than to act carelessly, simply because the bow was fully drawn and the target was waiting.

But never hold back from firing the arrow if all that paralyzes you is fear of making a mistake. If you have made the right movements, open your hand and release the string. Even if the arrow fails to hit the target, you will learn how to improve your aim next time.

If you never take a risk, you will never know what changes you need to make.

Each arrow leaves a memory in your heart, and it is the sum of those memories that will make you shoot better and better.

THE TARGET

The target is the objective to be reached.

It was chosen by the archer and though it is a long way off, we cannot blame it when we fail to hit it. In this lies the beauty of the way of the bow: you can never excuse yourself by saying that your opponent was stronger than you.

You were the one who chose the target and you are responsible for it.

The target can be larger, smaller, to the right or the left, but you always have to stand before it, respect it, and bring it closer mentally. Only when it is at the very end of your arrow should you release the bowstring.

If you view the target as the enemy, you might well hit the target, but you will not improve anything inside yourself. You will go through life trying only to place an arrow in the center of a piece of paper or wood, which is absolutely pointless. And when you are with other people, you will spend your time complaining that you never do anything interesting.

That is why you must choose your target, do your best to hit it, and always regard it with respect and dignity; you need to know what it means and how much effort, training, and intuition were required on your part.

When you look at the target, do not concentrate on that alone, but on everything going on around it, because the arrow, when it is shot, will encounter factors you failed to take into account, like wind, weight, and distance.

You must understand the target. You need to be constantly asking yourself: "If I am the target, where am I? How would it like to be hit, so as to give the archer the honor he deserves?"

The target exists only if the archer exists. What justifies its existence is the desire of the archer to hit it; otherwise it would be a mere inanimate object, an insignificant piece of paper or wood.

Just as the arrow seeks the target, so the target also seeks the arrow, because it is the arrow that gives meaning to its existence; it is no longer just a piece of paper; for an archer, it is the center of the world.

POSTURE

Once you have understood the bow, the arrow, and the target, you must have the serenity and elegance necessary to learn how to shoot.

Serenity comes from the heart. Although the heart is often tormented by thoughts of insecurity, it knows that—through correct posture—it will be able to do its best.

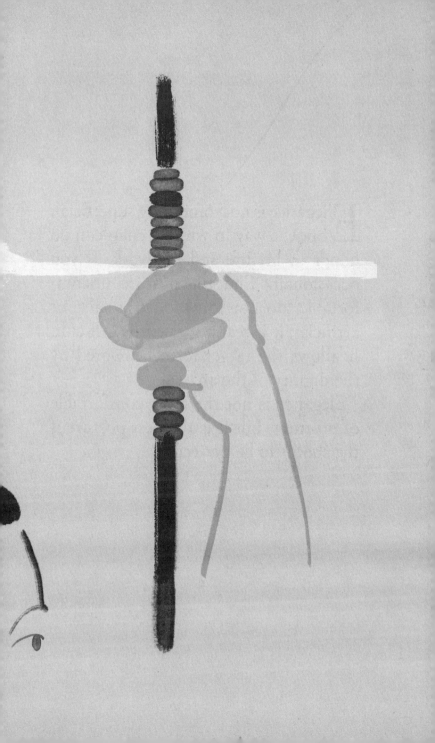

Elegance is not something superficial, but the way in which a man can do honor to his life and his work. If you occasionally find the posture uncomfortable, do not think of it as false or artificial; it is real because it is difficult. It allows the target to feel honored by the dignity of the archer.

Elegance is not the most comfortable of postures, but it is the best posture if the shot is to be perfect.

Elegance is achieved when everything superfluous has been discarded, and the archer discovers simplicity and concentration; the simpler and more sober the posture, the more beautiful.

The snow is lovely because it has only one color, the sea is lovely because it appears to be a completely flat surface, but both sea and snow are deep and know their own qualities.

How to Hold the Arrow

To hold the arrow is to be in touch with your own intention.

You must look along the whole length of the arrow, check that the feathers guiding its flight are well placed, and make sure that the point is sharp.

Ensure that it is straight and that it has not been bent or damaged by a previous shot.

In its simplicity and lightness, the arrow can appear fragile, but the strength of the archer means that it can carry the energy of his body and mind a long way. Legend has it that a single arrow once sank a ship, because the man who shot it knew where the wood was weakest and so made a hole that allowed the water to seep silently into the hold, thus putting an end to the threat of those would-be invaders of his village.

The arrow is the intention that leaves the archer's hand and sets off toward the target; that is, it is free in its flight and will follow the path chosen for it when it was released.

It will be affected by the wind and by gravity, but that is part of its trajectory; a leaf does not cease to be a leaf merely because a storm tore it from the tree.

A man's intention should be perfect, straight, sharp, firm, precise. No one can stop it as it crosses the space separating it from its destiny.

How to Hold the Bow

Keep calm and breathe deeply.
Every movement will be noticed by your allies, who will help you if necessary.

But do not forget that your opponent is watching you too, and he knows the difference between a steady hand and an unsteady one: therefore, if you are tense, breathe deeply, because that will help you to concentrate at every stage.

At the moment when you take up your bow and place it—elegantly—in front of your body, try to go over in your mind every stage that led up to the preparation of that shot.

But do this without tension, because it is impossible to hold all the rules in your head; and with a tranquil mind, as you review each stage, you will see again all the most difficult moments and how you overcame them.

This will give you confidence, and your hand will stop shaking.

How to Draw the Bowstring

The bow is a musical instrument, and its sound is made manifest in the string.

The bowstring is a big thing, but the arrow touches only one point on it, and all the archer's knowledge and experience should be concentrated on that one small point.

If he leans slightly to the right or to the left, if that point is above or below the line of fire, he will never hit the target.

Therefore, when you draw the bow-string, be like a musician playing an instrument. In music, time is more important than space; a group of notes on a line means nothing, but the person who can read what is written there can transform that line into sounds and rhythms.

Just as the archer justifies the existence of the target, so the arrow justifies the existence of the bow: you can throw an arrow with your hand, but a bow without an arrow is no use at all.

Therefore, when you open your arms, do not think of yourself as stretching the bow. Think of the arrow as the still center and that you are trying to bring the ends of the bow and bowstring closer together; touch the string delicately; ask for its cooperation.

How to Look at the Target

Many archers complain that, despite having practiced the art of archery for many years, they still feel their heart beating anxiously, their hands shaking, their aim failing. They need to understand that a bow or an arrow can change nothing, but that the art of archery makes our mistakes more obvious.

On a day when you are out of love with life, your aim will be confused, difficult. You will find that you lack the strength to draw the string back fully, that you cannot get the bow to bend as it should.

And when you see that your aim is poor that morning, you will try to find out what could have caused such imprecision; this will mean confronting the problem that is troubling you but that, up until then, has remained hidden.

The opposite can happen too: your aim is true; the string hums like a musical instrument; the birds are singing all around. Then you realize that you are giving of your best.

Nevertheless, do not allow yourself to be carried away by how you shoot in the morning, whether well or badly. There are many more days ahead, and each arrow is a life in itself.

Use your bad moments to discover what makes you tremble. Use your good moments to find your road to inner peace.

But do not stop either out of fear or out of joy: the way of the bow has no end.

The Moment of Release

There are two types of shot.

The first is the shot made with great precision, but without any soul. In this case, although the archer may have a great mastery of technique, he has concentrated solely on the target, and because of this he has not evolved, he has become stale, he has not managed to grow, and, one day, he will abandon the way of the bow because he finds that everything has become mere routine.

The second type of shot is the one made with the soul. When the intention of the archer is transformed into the flight of the arrow, his hand opens at the right moment, the sound of the string makes the birds sing, and the gesture of shooting something over a distance provokes—paradoxically enough—a return to and an encounter with oneself.

You know the effort it took to draw the bow, to breathe correctly, to concentrate on the target, to be clear about your intention, to maintain elegance of posture, to respect the target, but you need to understand too that nothing in this world stays with us for very long: at a given moment, your hand will have to open and allow your intention to follow its destiny.

Therefore, the arrow must leave, however much you love all the steps that led to the elegant posture and the correct intention, and however much you admire its feathers, its point, its shape.

However, it cannot leave before the archer is ready to shoot, because its flight would be too brief.

It cannot leave after the exact posture and concentration have been achieved, because the body would be unable to withstand the effort and the hand would begin to shake.

It must leave at the moment when bow, archer, and target are at the same point in the universe: this is called inspiration.

Repetition

The gesture is the incarnation of the verb; that is, an action is a thought made manifest.

A small gesture betrays us, so we must polish everything, think about details, learn the technique in such a way that it becomes intuitive. Intuition has nothing to do with routine, but with a state of mind that is beyond technique.

So, after much practicing, we no longer think about the necessary movements; they become part of our own existence. But for this to happen, you must practice and repeat.

And if that isn't enough, you must repeat and practice.

Look at the skilled farrier working steel. To the untrained eye, he is merely repeating the same hammer blows.

But anyone who knows the way of the bow knows that each time he lifts the hammer and brings it down, the intensity of the blow is different. The hand repeats the same gesture, but as it approaches the metal, it understands that it must touch it with more or less force.

So it is with repetition; although it may appear to be the same thing, it is always different.

Look at the windmill. To someone who glances at its sails only once, they seem to be moving at the same speed, repeating the same movement.

But those familiar with windmills know that they are controlled by the wind and change direction as necessary.

The hand of the farrier was trained by repeating the gesture of hammering thousands of times. The sails of the windmill can move fast when the wind blows hard and thus ensure that its gears run smoothly.

The archer allows many arrows to go far beyond the target, because he knows that he will learn the importance of bow, posture, string, and target only by repeating his gestures thousands of times and by not being afraid of making mistakes.

And his true allies will never criticize him, because they know that practice is necessary, that it is the only way in which he can perfect his instinct, his hammer blow.

And then comes the moment when he no longer has to think about what he is doing. From then on, the archer becomes his bow, his arrow, and his target.

How to Observe the
Flight of the Arrow

Once the arrow has been shot, there is nothing more the archer can do, except follow its path to the target. From that moment on, the tension required to shoot the arrow has no further reason to exist.

Therefore, the archer keeps his eyes fixed on the flight of the arrow, but his heart rests, and he smiles.

The hand that released the bowstring is thrust back; the hand holding the bow moves forward; the archer is forced to open wide his arms and confront, chest exposed and with a sincere heart, the gaze of both allies and opponents.

If he has practiced enough, if he has managed to develop his instinct, if he has maintained elegance and concentration throughout the whole process of shooting the arrow, he will, at that moment, feel the presence of the universe and will see that his action was just and deserved.

Technique allows both hands to be ready, breathing to be precise, the eyes to be trained on the target. Instinct allows the moment of release to be perfect.

Anyone passing nearby and seeing the archer with his arms open, his eyes following the arrow, will think that nothing is happening. But his allies know that the mind of the person who made the shot has changed dimensions; it is now in touch with the whole universe.

The mind continues to work, learning all the positive things about that shot, correcting possible errors, accepting its good qualities, and waiting to see how the target reacts when it is hit.

When the archer draws the bowstring, he can see the whole world in his bow.

When he follows the flight of the arrow, that world grows closer to him, caresses him, and gives him a perfect sense of duty fulfilled.

Each arrow flies differently. You can shoot a thousand arrows and each one will follow a different trajectory: that is the way of the bow.

The Archer Without Bow, Without Arrow, Without Target

The archer learns when he forgets all about the rules of the way of the bow and goes on to act entirely on instinct. In order, though, to be able to forget the rules, it is necessary to respect them and to know them.

When he reaches this state, he no longer needs the instruments that helped him to learn. He no longer needs the bow or the arrows or the target, because the path is more important than the thing that first set him on that path.

In the same way, the student learning to read reaches a point when he frees himself from the individual letters and begins to make words out of them.

However, if the words were all run together, they would make no sense at all or would make understanding extremely hard; there have to be spaces between the words.

Between one action and the next, the archer remembers everything he has done; he talks with his allies; he rests and is content with the fact of being alive.

The way of the bow is the way of joy and enthusiasm, of perfection and error, of technique and instinct.

"But you will only learn this if you keep shooting your arrows."

Epilogue

By the time Tetsuya stopped talking, they had reached the carpentry workshop.

"Thank you for your company," he said to the boy.

But the boy did not leave.

"How can I know if I'm doing the right thing? How can I be sure that my eyes are concentrating, that my posture is elegant, that I'm holding the bow correctly?"

"Visualize the perfect master always by your side, and do everything to revere him and to honor his teachings. This master, whom many people call God, although some call him 'the thing' and others 'talent,' is always watching us.

"He deserves the best.

"Remember your allies too: you must support them, because they will help you at those moments when you need help. Try to develop the gift of kindness: this gift will allow you to be always at peace with your heart. But, above all, never forget that what I have told you might perhaps be words of inspiration, but they will make sense only if you experience them yourself."

Tetsuya held out his hand to say goodbye, but the boy said:

"One other thing: How did you learn to shoot a bow?"

Tetsuya thought for a moment: Was it worth telling the story? Since this had been a special day, he opened the door to his workshop and said:

"I'm going to make some tea, and I'm going to tell you the story, but you have to promise the same thing I made the stranger promise—never tell anyone about my skill as an archer."

He went in, put on the light, wrapped his bow up again in the long strip of leather and placed it out of sight. If anyone stumbled upon it, they would think it was just a piece of warped bamboo. He went into the kitchen, made the tea, sat down with the boy, and began his story.

"I was working for a great nobleman who lived in the region; I was in charge of looking after his stables. But since my master was always traveling, I had a great deal of free time, and so I decided to devote myself to what I considered to be the real reason for living: drink and women.

"One day, after several nights without sleep, I felt dizzy and collapsed in the middle of the countryside, far from anywhere. I thought I was going to die and gave up all hope. However, a man I had never seen before happened to pass along that road; he helped me and took me to his house—a place far from here—and nursed me back to health during the months that followed. While I was recovering, I used to see him set out every morning with his bow and arrows.

"When I felt better, I asked him to teach me the art of the bow; it was far more interesting than looking after horses. He told me that my death had come a great deal closer, and that now I could not drive it away. It was just two paces away from me, for I had done great physical harm to my body.

"If I wanted to learn, it would only be in order to keep death from touching me. A man in a far-off land, on the other side of the ocean, had taught him that it was possible to avoid for some time the road that led to the precipice of death. But in my case, for the rest of my days, I needed to be aware that I was walking along the edge of this abyss and could fall into it at any moment.

"He taught me the way of the bow. He introduced me to his allies, he made me take part in competitions, and soon my fame spread throughout the land.

"When he saw that I had learned enough, he took away my arrows and my target, leaving me only the bow as a souvenir. He told me to use his teachings to do something that filled me with real enthusiasm.

"I said that the thing I liked most was carpentry. He blessed me and asked me to leave and to devote myself to what I enjoyed doing most before my fame as an archer ended up destroying me, or led me back to my former life.

"Every second since then has been a struggle against my vices and against self-pity. I need to remain focused and calm, to do the work I chose to do with love, and never to cling to the present moment, because death is still very close, the abyss is there beside me, and I am walking along the edge."

Tetsuya did not say that death is always close for all living beings; the boy was still very young and there was no need for him to think about such things.

Tetsuya did not say either that the way

of the bow is present in any human activity.

He merely blessed the boy, just as he had been blessed many years before, and asked him to leave, because it had been a long day, and he needed to sleep.

Acknowledgments

To Eugen Herrigel, for his book **Zen in the Art of Archery,** Derby Editions, 2016.

To Pamela Hartigan, managing director of the Schwab Foundation for Social Entrepreneurship, for describing the qualities of allies.

To Dan and Jackie DeProspero, for their book with Onuma-san, **Kyudo,** Budo Editions.

To Carlos Castaneda, for his description of the encounter between death and the **nagual** Elias.

A NOTE ABOUT THE AUTHOR

Paulo Coelho's life remains the primary source of inspiration for his books. He has flirted with death, escaped madness, dallied with drugs, withstood torture, experimented with magic and alchemy, studied philosophy and religion, read voraciously, lost and recovered his faith, and experienced the pain and pleasure of love. In searching for his own place in the world, he has discovered answers for the challenges that everyone faces. He believes that, within ourselves, we have the necessary strength to find our own destiny.

Paulo Coelho's books have been translated into 82 languages and have sold more than 320 million copies in more than 170 countries. His 1998 novel **The Alchemist** has sold more than 85 million copies and has been cited as an inspiration by people as diverse as Malala Yousafzai and Pharrell Williams.

He is a member of the Brazilian Academy of Letters and has received the Chevalier de l'Ordre National de la Légion d'Honneur. In 2007, he was named a United Nations Messenger of Peace.

A NOTE ABOUT THE ILLUSTRATOR

Born in Waiblingen, Germany, Christoph Niemann is an artist, author, and animator. His work appears regularly on the covers of **The New Yorker, National Geographic,** and **The New York Times Magazine.** Christoph Niemann's art has been subject to numerous museum retrospectives. He created **The New Yorker**'s first Augmented Reality Cover. In 2010, he was inducted into the Art Directors Club Hall of Fame. He is the author of many books, including the monographs **Sunday Sketching** (2016), **WORDS** (2016), and **Souvenir** (2017). His most recent book is **Hopes and Dreams** about a trip to meet an artistic hero in Los Angeles. He lives in Berlin with his family.

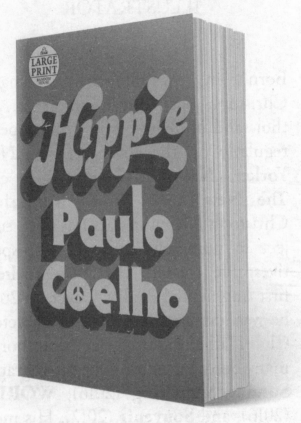